Costume Party

by Miriam Sklar

ISBN: 978-1-338-75074-4
Illustrated by John Lund

Published by Scholastic Inc., 557 Broadway, New York, NY 10012

10 9 8 7 6 5 4 68 25 26 27/0

Printed in Jiaxing, China. First printing, January 2021.

I may be a witch.

I may be a fish.

I may be a bee.

I may be a tree.

I may be a fox.

I may be a clock.

I may be a box!